Monster Beneath my Bed

by Tiffany A. Higgins

illustrated by Clark L. Higgins

This book is for everyone who has ever been afraid of what is there in the dark.

This story is Alexandra's story. Her fears, her experiences and her discoveries are what made this story possible. The ending is her ending.

We hope that everyone finds their monsters to be as easy to cope with as the monster beneath her bed.

Remember, what's there in the dark is the same thing as what was there in the light.

"There's a monster beneath my bed!" I said

Daddy just smiles and shakes his head.

I hear it moving while I sleep.

Thud

Bump

Scratch

I try so hard not to make a peep.

But when the sun comes up at last,

the monster must run really fast.

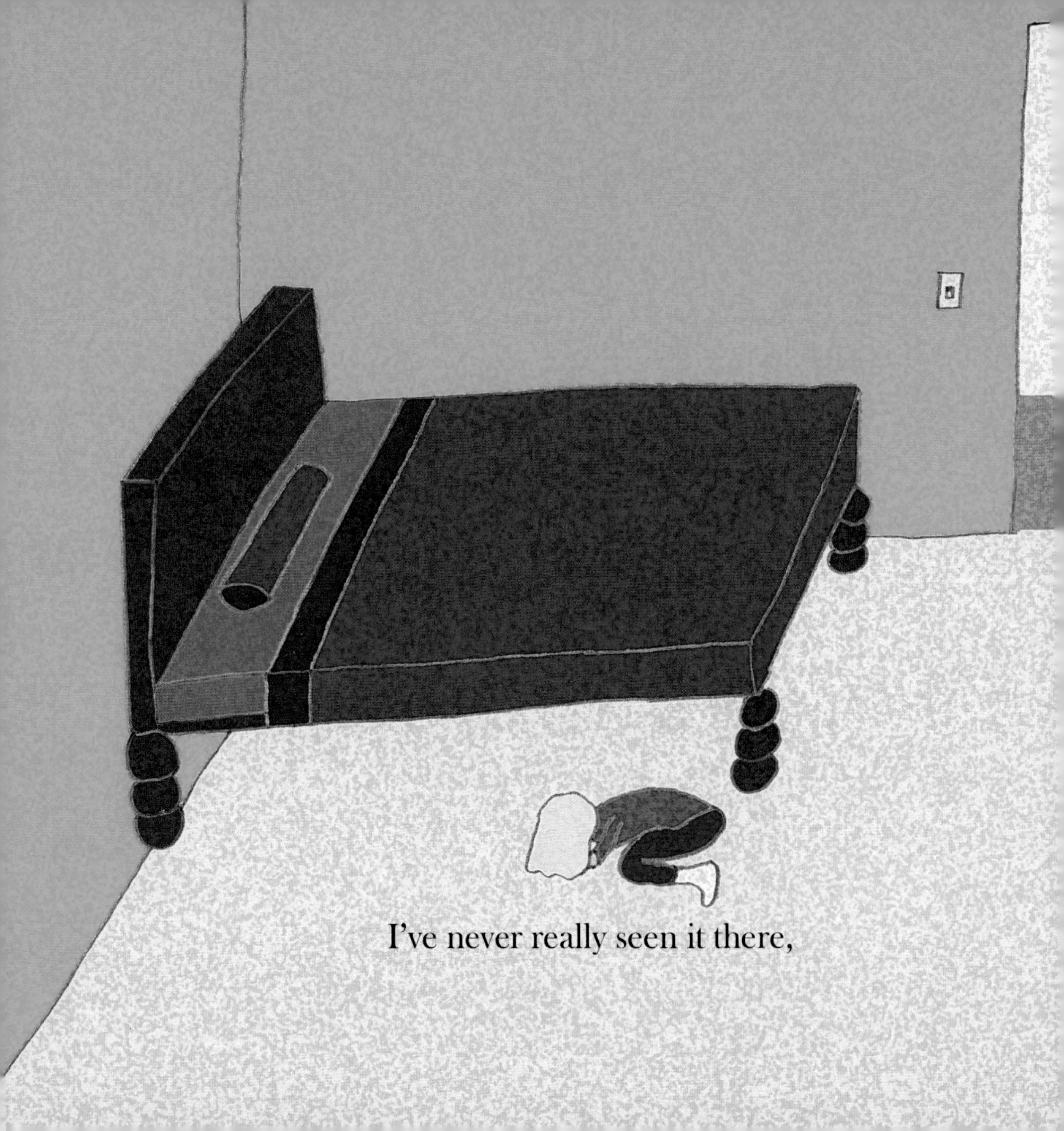
I’ve never really seen it there,

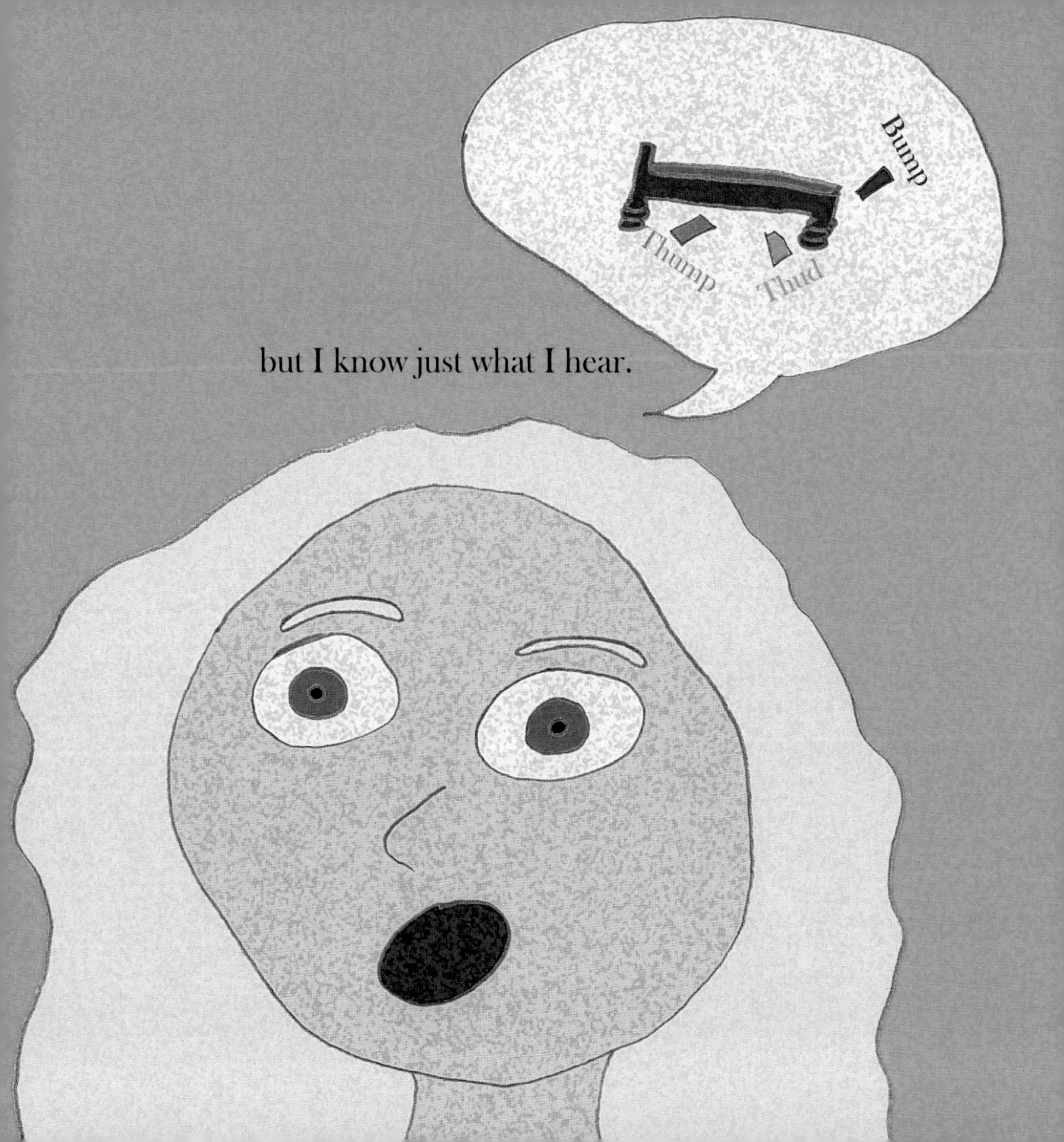
but I know just what I hear.
Thump
Thud
Bump

Under my bed, there
lives a monster.

But during the day, he does not stir.

When my daddy
tucks me in.

he turns to me with a huge grin.

"I've found your monster under there."

"I bet he sure gave you a scare."

“Why don’t you come and look,
you’ll see,”

"before this monster decides to flee."

I slowly climb down to the floor.

It’s just my kitten and nothing more.

Tee Hee Hee

Ha Ha Ha Ha

I start to giggle, and then I laugh.
Imagine that,

My monster was only my cat.

If you enjoyed *Monster Beneath my Bed*,

check out these other titles by

Tiffany A. & Clark L. Higgins

We've Seen Santa

Follow a brother and sister as they sneak down on Christmas Eve
to catch Santa in the act.

I Love the Changing Seasons

Explores the changing weather and activities
that make each season unique.

Find us on Facebook

Facebook.com/Tiffany.and.Clark.Higgins.Books

Made in the USA
Monee, IL
02 May 2023